CRACKERJACK
HALFBACK

CRACKERJACK
HALFBACK

by Matt Christopher

Illustrated by Karen Meyer

 Little, Brown and Company
Boston   New York   Toronto   London

First Paperback Edition.

ISBN 0-316-13728-6

Library of Congress catalog card number 62-12372

10 9 8 7 6 5 4 3 2 1

COM-MO

Published simultaneously in Canada by Little, Brown &
Company (Canada) Limited

Printed in the United States of America

To Mike and Jean

CRACKERJACK HALFBACK

1

The warm Saturday morning sun beat down on the fans filling the bleachers that lined one side of the eighty-yard football field. It beat down on Freddie Chase's back as he crouched in position behind right guard and right tackle.

The Sandpipers, dressed in bright yellow uniforms, formed a tight line as they faced the green-uniformed Catbirds. The ball was on the two-yard line, and the Catbirds were trying for the extra point.

"One! Two! Hike!"

The quarterback took the snap, turned, and handed it off to the fullback. The fullback tucked the ball against his chest and charged toward the right side of the Sandpipers' line. Freddie plunged forward, closing the narrow hole that split open between right guard Harry Lott and right tackle Steve Cook.

But all at once a white helmet with a bird painted on its front hit him on the chest. He bounced back like a rubber ball. A whistle pierced the air, and Freddie saw the boy in the white helmet sprawled over the goal line.

The Catbirds scrambled excitedly to their feet and let out a lusty yell.

"That's fourteen for them," Dick Connors said sourly. He was captain and quarterback for the Sandpipers. "What are we going to do — lose every game this year, too?"

Freddie knew exactly how Dick felt. The Sandpipers hadn't won a game in two years. A very sad record, indeed. The first league games of the season had been played last week, and the Sandpipers had lost theirs to the Flamingos, 21–7.

So far, in today's game, the Sandpipers had been doing better. Freddie, who played both offense and defense, had set up a touchdown play in the first quarter by intercepting a pass. He had run twenty yards before a Catbird had brought him down. On the next play Dick had faked a handoff to Freddie, at right halfback, then passed to right end Milt Grady. Milt went over for the touchdown, and fullback Dennis Yates bucked for the extra point.

But the Catbirds had one of the speediest fullbacks in the league, Ernie Moody. Every time he carried the ball he gained ground. He had a funny habit. He was always smiling and clapping his hands. Freddie had thought that Ernie was doing this to keep warm, until he realized that after running around so much Ernie really didn't have to clap his hands anymore. But Ernie kept on doing it, and Freddie knew then that it was just Ernie's way.

The teams lined up for the kickoff. The referee signaled for the game to start, and Ernie Moody kicked off for the Catbirds.

Dick Connors caught the end-over-end boot on his twenty-yard line and carried it to his thirty-five.

Quick as light he leaped to his feet. "Huddle!" he said.

While they were in the huddle, two players pushed themselves into the group.

Freddie tensed. So far he had been pulled out of the game for only a few minutes in the first quarter. He didn't know why, except that he knew Coach Hank Sears believed in playing every boy.

"Steve and Dave — out!" one of the substitutes said.

Freddie breathed easier.

"Crisscross buck," said Dick. "Bucky takes it. On the two!"

The team broke out of the huddle and scrambled to the line of scrimmage. The Sandpipers used the T-formation, a seven-man line with the quarterback directly behind the center, the fullback directly in line behind the quarterback, and the halfbacks on either side of him.

The play skipped swiftly through Freddie's mind. He wished he carried, though, instead of Bucky.

"Down!" snapped quarterback Dick Connors. "One! Two! Hike!"

Center Stookie Freese snapped the ball. Dick took it and spun around. Freddie shot crosswise in front of him and reached for the ball. Then he pulled his arms against him, as if he had the ball, and rushed through the hole between left guard and tackle.

Right after Freddie did his part, Bucky Jensen raced crosswise in front of Dick from his left halfback position. Dick pushed the ball into Bucky's arms, and Bucky plunged through the hole between right guard and tackle. He kept going, dodging and leaping just out of reach of would-be tacklers. Then a linebacker pulled him down on the Catbirds' thirty-nine.

Second down and four yards to go.

Dick grinned as the boys huddled again. "Nice going, Bucky. Let's try it again. Only this time Freddie carries. On the three!"

Freddie's heart pounded as the team broke from the huddle. This was what he loved more than anything—running with the ball. It was very seldom that Dick gave him the chance.

"Down!" ordered Dick. "One! Two! Three! Hike!"

The ball snapped. Helmets clattered as they smacked against each other. Yellow and green jerseys mixed like a bowl of tossed salad. And then a marker was dropped and a whistle shrilled.

The referee was striking his hips with his hands.

The offside signal! And it was against the Catbirds!

Freddie leaped happily.

Now the ball was on the Catbirds' thirty-four-yard line. It was first and ten.

"The same play," said Dick in the huddle.

Freddie took the handoff from Dick and plunged through the hole in the left side of the line. He ran hard, the football gripped tightly against him. Then he was hit. He went down, and it seemed as if the whole Catbirds line was piled on top of him. When it got off, he rose to his feet.

"Second down and six," said the referee.

Dick suggested a pass play. On "Hike!" Dick stepped quickly back with the ball. He faked to Freddie, who ran to the left. Then Dick heaved a long, spiraling pass toward the left side of the field. It was intended for Bucky.

Suddenly a player in green pulled the ball out of the air and started running with it the other way!

A bit of fear went through Freddie. The player was running along the sideline. There was nobody between him and the goal line except Freddie: Only Freddie could get to the Catbird runner and stop him from making a touchdown.

Freddie started to run. He recognized the man in green now. It was Ernie Moody, the Catbirds'

star player. Even now Ernie seemed to be smiling that silly smile of his, and saying, *Come on, kid! I dare you to tackle me!*

"Get him, Freddie!" a voice shouted. "Get him!"

But as Freddie drew near to Ernie and saw how hard Ernie was running and how high his knees rose with every step, that bit of fear grew into mountainous size.

He reached out for Ernie, standing up instead of diving at Ernie's legs as he should have. Ernie stiff-armed him and drove him back so that he almost went sprawling.

Ernie galloped on for the touchdown.

A roar sprang from the Catbirds' fans. Then Ernie bucked for the extra point. He didn't make it.

A moment later a harsh voice snapped at Freddie's elbow: "Out, Freddie. The coach has something to say to you!"

2

Freddie hardly glanced at Ted Butler, who replaced him. He lowered his head and raced off the field.

Coach Hank Sears met him at the sideline. He towered over Freddie like a skyscraper, his dark hair whipping in the wind.

"Freddie! You let him go by! You didn't even try to tackle him!"

Freddie made no reply. He kept his eyes at a level with the coach's belt.

"Freddie!" Mr. Sears's voice lowered a pitch. "I saw you do that same thing in our game against the Flamingos last week. I thought then that you were afraid to tackle. I wasn't sure."

So Mr. Sears had noticed. Now he'd realize that Freddie wasn't the wonderful backfield man he had expected him to be. What kind of a backfield man was he, if he was afraid to tackle?

"Sit down, Freddie," said the coach. "Rest."

From the bench, Freddie watched Ernie boot the ball far into the Sandpipers' territory. Fullback Dennis Yates caught it and ran it back to his thirty-two.

Freddie wondered if he'd get a chance to go in again. He wouldn't be afraid to tackle the next time. He promised himself that.

But hadn't he promised himself that before? Dozens and dozens of times. And just when he'd have to make a tackle, what happened? He'd get scared all over and the runner would race right past him!

If he was going to play defensive linebacker as well as offensive halfback, he'd have to get over that fear — soon.

The half ended. The Sandpipers went off to one side of the field, and the Catbirds went off to the other.

Coach Sears talked to the boys awhile, telling them what they had done wrong and what they should have done. Freddie kept behind some of the bigger boys — the tackles and the guards — so that Coach Sears wouldn't notice him and say something about his not tackling. He felt sure some of the boys knew, but if Coach Sears broadcast it now — well, he just wouldn't be able to take it, that's what.

They returned to the bench and talked to pass the rest of the minutes.

Freddie was still sitting there when the second half started. Dennis kicked off. It was Ernie Moody again who caught the ball on his twenty and ran it back. He got as far as his twenty-eight, where Dick Connors and end Milt Grady smeared him.

The Catbirds gained a first down in three plays. Freddie began to fidget on the bench. He couldn't forget that he was to blame for the Catbirds' getting the last touchdown.

And then — on the Sandpipers' thirty-three — the Catbirds fumbled the ball and the Sandpipers recovered!

Freddie leaped off the bench with joy, practically forgetting why he was there.

"Freddie, get in there," barked Coach Sears. "Send out Ted."

Freddie looked up at the coach. "Did you —"

"Will you hurry?" said Coach Sears. "We haven't got all day."

"Yes, sir!" replied Freddie. He clipped on his chin strap and raced out onto the field.

He ordered Ted Butler out and saw the looks that came over the faces of the other players. Especially Dick Connors's, the captain, and fullback Dennis Yates's.

"Pass to Milt," said Dick. "On the two! Let's go!" They broke from the huddle and went quickly into a T-formation. Dick, his hands stretched down close to center Stookie Freese's legs, barked signals.

"Down! One! Two! Hike!"

Stookie snapped the ball. Dick took it and went back. He faked a handoff to Dennis, then shot a forward pass across the scrimmage line toward the right side of the field. Milt caught it, went five yards, and was tackled.

"Second and two!" said the referee.

The Sandpipers' fans began yelling: "We — want — a touchdown! We — want — a touchdown!"

Dick tried a crisscross buck, with Bucky carrying. They lost two yards. Third and four.

14

"Let me carry it!" said Freddie.

All eyes swung to him, big and wide and unbelieving.

"They — they won't expect it," said Freddie timidly.

Ten pairs of eyes kept staring at him.

Then Dick said, "Okay! It might surprise them! If you don't make it, we'll still have another down! Number twelve! Block your men, you guys!"

Dick snapped signals. The ball whipped into his hands. He ran with it toward the right side of the line. A tackle broke through and started after him. Dennis blocked him. An end broke through. He reached for Dick. Just then Dick pitched the ball out to Freddie, who was running hard alongside him.

Freddie clamped the ball tightly against his side and raced hard down the field. Coming from his left was the Catbirds' safety man. Freddie tried to pick up more speed. He was on the fifteen, now . . . the ten . . . the five. . . .

The safety man reached him, grabbed his shoulders, and pulled him down. Just three yards from the goal line!

"Beautiful run, Freddie!" praised Dick. "Let's go for it now. I'll try the sneak."

Dick tried it, and plunged through for the touchdown.

Dennis bucked from the two. He didn't make it.

The score: Catbirds 20; Sandpipers 13.

The coach sent in substitutes. One was Ted Butler, who came in again to replace Freddie.

"Nice running, Freddie," said Coach Sears with a smile. "I think I know what to do with you now."

Freddie gazed at him with puzzlement, then looked away. What did the coach mean by that?

The third quarter ended, and the teams switched goals. The Catbirds moved into Sandpipers territory. Then Ernie Moody heaved a long forward pass. Fullback Mike Polski, who had gone in for Dennis, intercepted it. He ran it back to the thirty-eight, where he was downed.

"Get in there, Freddie," snapped the coach. "On the double!"

Freddie ran in.

"Let me take it!" he said in the huddle.

Dick glared at him. "In case you didn't know," he said gruffly, "I'm captain."

Freddie blushed. He wanted to tell Dick and the others that all he wanted was to make up for the touchdown he had given the Catbirds. But there was no way he could say that.

"Pass to Mills," said Dick. "On the three!"

Dick passed. Left end Joey Mills overran the ball, and it was incomplete.

"Try it to me this time," pleaded Freddie.

"You heard me!" said Dick, his eyes hot as they pierced the little right halfback's. "We'll try it again, but this time to Milt."

Milt was off at the snap. So was Freddie. He raced down the field, running about two yards inside of Milt. He saw the Catbirds' linebackers chasing after them. Ahead was their safety man, charging forward.

Suddenly the ball came spiraling through the air like a pointed torpedo. It soared over Freddie's head. Milt caught it, stumbled, and went on. He was out of danger from the linebackers. But the safety man was almost upon him.

Just as the safety man lunged for Milt, Freddie shouted, "Here, Milt! Behind you!"

Milt flipped the ball behind him. It struck the tips of Freddie's fingers and almost dropped. Then he pulled it against his side and ran on. The white stripes slipped underneath him, until he crossed the goal line.

Seconds later, Dennis bucked for the extra point, and the score was tied: 20–20.

3

The game ended a little while later with the score locked at 20–20. Freddie took off his helmet and let the wind cool his head. He had started homeward when he heard someone running up behind him.

"Hey, Cuz! See you guys finally tied a game!"

His cousin Mert McGuire came up behind him and clapped him hard on the back.

"At least we didn't lose," replied Freddie.

Mert played fullback for the Cardinals, the team that had won the championship the last two years. He was tall and fast and easily the best player in the league. Freddie had to admit that the Cardinals would not be much of a team without him. But Freddie would never tell that to Mert, even if Mert was his cousin.

"You can travel with that ball," said Mert, "but you have a weakness. I saw it."

Freddie slapped his helmet against his thigh. The sun was overhead and behind the two boys, so that their shadows walked along in front of them. Freddie's shoulder pads made his shadow look almost twice as broad as Mert's, who was wearing a sweater.

"Did Coach Sears tell you?" said Mert.

The shadow of his chin jutted toward Freddie's wide right shoulder. Suddenly Freddie lifted his shoulder, and his shadow came up and smacked the shadow of Mert's chin.

Freddie ignored Mert's question.

"How did the Flamingos make out?" he asked.

The Flamingos had played that morning on the A field, which adjoined the B field, where the Sandpipers had played. This arrangement made it possible for two games to be played every Saturday morning, with one in the afternoon.

"They lost," answered Mert. "The Owls beat them thirty-one to twenty-six." A wiseacre smile came over Mert's face. "You sure have a weakness, Freddie. A very bad weakness. It's no use hiding it.

Everybody knows, especially your coach. Bet he makes some roster changes soon!"

Freddie's heart throbbed. A car went by and the horn tooted. He recognized some of the boys on the team sitting in the backseat—Dick Connors, Mike Polski, Joey Mills.

"Guys break through you like water," Mert went on. "You'd better not play when your team plays us. I'd hate to spill you with a stiff-arm."

Freddie tried to swallow his anger. He looked at Mert. "That's a long time away. Anything could happen by then."

"I know," said Mert, smiling. "You could lose every game! Ha ha! So long, Cuz! This is where I turn off!"

Why do I have to have a cousin like him? thought Freddie. He wished he had poked Mert's chin shadow once more while he had had the chance.

He arrived home and found his mom busily vacuuming the living room rug. She was tall, and pretty, even with her hair in curlers. Since his dad had died, she worked during the week in an office and used Saturday to do her housecleaning.

She saw him walk in the door and smiled. She stepped on a lever on the vacuum cleaner, and it whirred to a stop.

"Well!" she said. "Who won?"

"We tied," Freddie replied. "Twenty-twenty. I'm hungry, Mom. Got anything to eat?"

"In a minute," she said. "Change your clothes and wash up." She frowned then. "Your uniform looks pretty clean. Didn't you play?"

He looked away and felt himself blush. "I played some," he mumbled, and walked to his bedroom, where he started to change out of his uniform.

She wouldn't have said that if she'd gone to the game. Hadn't he made some long runs with the ball? Hadn't he scored that last touchdown?

He showered and changed.

Mom was unplugging the electric cord when he came out. "Put this away for me, will you, Freddie? I'll get lunch for us."

He wound the long cord around the cleaner, then put the cleaner away in a closet.

"I just remembered," said Mom. "Jimmie Rose was here a little while ago. He wants you to play with him."

Freddie's brows arched. "Jimmie Rose?"

She smiled. "Yes. He wants to play football with you."

"But I just got through playing football!" murmured Freddie.

"I know. But after lunch, can't you play with him just a little? He likes you a lot, you know."

"Yeah, I know," said Freddie.

And then he thought, Maybe I can tackle Jimmie. He's a lot younger than I am. And a lot smaller.

4

After lunch, Mom told Freddie he'd better rest awhile before going to Jimmie's.

"Don't want you to get a stomachache," she said.

He put on his tan windbreaker and his cap, went out, and sat on the front porch. The sun shone like a thousand glittering diamonds through the tall elm tree standing inside the curb. It speckled him with shadows.

He got to thinking. He didn't especially care about playing with Jimmie; Jimmie was too small. Still, he'd never seen a boy quite like Jimmie. Jimmie had more "pep, zip, and vinegar" than anybody Freddie knew.

When he decided that his food had digested enough, he got up and went to Jimmie's. Jimmie lived half a block down the street.

Freddie walked around the large, white house to the backyard. Sure enough, a little boy with very wide shoulders and big numbers on the back of his green jersey was playing with a football. The boy was also wearing a black football helmet with a white stripe through the middle of it, and a face guard.

"Hi, Jimmie," Freddie said.

Jimmie turned. A grin spread like sunshine across his face.

"Hi, Freddie!" Then disappointment wiped away the smile. "Where's your uniform and helmet?"

Freddie shrugged. "Took them off. I played this morning."

Jimmie came up to him, the football pressed under his arm. "Will you still play with me, please? In the park across the street? There's more room there."

Freddie thought about it a minute. Jimmie was so little! Why didn't he ask some kid his own size?

"I just finished eating," he said, making an excuse.

"That's all right," replied Jimmie. The disappointment faded quickly from his face. "You don't have to run much. Come on!"

Jimmie raced ahead of him out of the yard. Near the street he stopped, watched for cars, then ran across to the park. Freddie shrugged. What could he do? He trotted after Jimmie.

He was glad that the park was empty.

Jimmie passed the football to him, then ran in the opposite direction, waiting for Freddie to throw. Freddie tossed a spiral, and Jimmie caught it over his shoulder.

That kid! thought Freddie. He's small, but great!

"Let's play tackle," Jimmie suggested after a while.

"Tackle?" Freddie echoed. "Who — you and me?"

"Sure!" said Jimmie seriously. "You hike and I'll run. If I don't make a TD in four downs, then it's your turn."

Freddie stared. "A TD?"

"Of course!" replied Jimmie. "A touchdown! That big tree there is the goal line." That Jimmie was just fantastic!

Then all at once Freddie remembered some of the things that had happened in the game that morning, and a strange feeling came over him.

"Let's play touch tackle," he suggested. "Then nobody will get hurt."

"Get hurt?" Jimmie frowned as if that was the last thing he would think of. "Not me! I have my shoulder pads on, and my helmet! Want to go home and get yours?"

Listen to him! thought Freddie. I'm making him think I'm afraid! I can't do that!

He forced a smile to his lips. "No, never mind," he said. "Okay. You call signals."

Jimmie tossed him the ball. Freddie held it on the ground, and Jimmie began yelling signals: "Four! Two! Five! Hike!"

At the word "Hike!" Freddie centered the ball to Jimmie. Jimmie caught it and started running past Freddie. He tried to stiff-arm Freddie. Laughing, Freddie reached out and pulled Jimmie gently to the ground.

"Gained a little!" said Jimmie. "Second down!"

Suddenly loud applause sounded behind them. "Way to go, Freddie! Nice tackle!"

Freddie spun. Coming toward them were two of his teammates, Harry Lott and Steve Cook. Freddie's face turned tomato red.

"See who he picks on?" Harry said. "Little kids!"

"Naturally," said Steve. "He doesn't dare tackle anybody his size."

They both roared with laughter.

Freddie stood frozen. Now he knew he should not have come here with Jimmie.

"Go home," said Jimmie. "Leave us alone."

Harry chuckled. He played right guard and was a first-stringer on the team. "Let me see that ball, kid."

Jimmie wrapped both arms around the ball. "I will not. You heard me. I said go home!"

Harry chuckled again. He went up to Jimmie. Jimmie backed away, then quickly passed the ball to Freddie. Steve jumped in front of it and caught it. He and Harry began throwing it back and forth, teasing Jimmie and Freddie.

"Give me back my ball!" cried Jimmie angrily. "Help me, Freddie!"

Freddie's heart pounded. Those bullies, he thought.

Both Harry and Steve laughed at the way they teased the two smaller boys. The more Freddie and Jimmie tried to get the ball, the louder the boys laughed.

Then, just as Steve passed the ball again to Harry, Jimmie ran across the ground and dived at Harry's legs.

Down went Harry, the ball squirting from his hands!

Quickly Freddie picked it up. He pulled it firmly against him, then stepped back and looked at Steve. But Steve wasn't moving. He was looking directly at the two boys on the ground, looking as if he couldn't believe what he saw.

Jimmie got up. And then slowly Harry got up. He brushed the dirt from his pants.

"Come on, Steve," he said, his face a little red. "Let's go."

Freddie stared at their backs as they left. Then he stared at Jimmie . . . at the little kid who had tackled big Harry Lott.

5

Ms. Daley, Freddie's teacher, gave the class an arithmetic test on Monday morning. Freddie enjoyed arithmetic. He liked to figure out problems, but this morning he just could not concentrate on what he was doing.

Several boys in school had heard about his playing football with little Jimmie Rose. Harry and Steve had told them about it. One of the boys was Dick Connors, the Sandpipers' quarterback — and Dick was in Freddie's class.

"I heard you really gave Jimmie a spill," Dick had said first thing this morning. "He's so *big*. How did you ever get the nerve?"

Dick wasn't one to tease very often. That was why Freddie could not forget his remark. It stayed with him like an itch he couldn't scratch.

When the arithmetic test was over, the students passed their papers to their neighbors across the aisles. Miss Daley then read off the answers, and everyone marked the papers. When the papers were all marked, they were returned to their owners.

Freddie looked unhappily at his mark: 84. He knew he could have done better. He would have, too, if he could have concentrated.

By the time noon rolled around, he felt better. In history class, he put up his hand almost every time Ms. Daley asked a question. Whenever he was called on, he answered the question correctly, too.

After school, he went home, dressed in his football uniform, and went to the field. It was the first time he had ever hated to go to football practice; he was afraid of the greeting he'd receive. He purposely avoided Harry, Steve, and Dick — but then he noticed Harry walking away from *him*. Could Harry be thinking about Jimmie's tackling him, and was he embarrassed about it in front of Freddie?

"Okay!" said Coach Sears. "We're going to try some signal drills. First team, line up!"

Freddie stood back. He wasn't sure if he was on the first team now or not.

"Come on, Freddie," Coach Sears said to him suddenly. "Get in right half."

They went into a T-formation, with Joey Mills at left end, Dave Summers at left tackle, Ken Wallace at left guard, and Stookie Freese at center. At the right side of the line were Harry Lott at guard, Steve Cook at tackle, and Milt Grady at end. In the backfield were Dick Connors in the quarterback slot and behind him left halfback Bucky Jensen, fullback Dennis Yates, and right halfback Freddie.

"Huddle!" yelled Coach Sears.

In the huddle, the coach suggested a crisscross buck, with Bucky carrying. Later they tried laterals, as well as plays with Dick handing off to Dennis, or sometimes to Freddie or to one of the ends, Joey and Milt. Milt proved a good receiver for Dick's long forward passes.

Several times Harry and Dave started off too quickly, and the coach warned them for being offside, a five-yard penalty in a game.

Then Coach Sears had the second team work on defense against the first. After that he had them all stand in a double line. The player in the right-hand line would run forward, and the player in the left-hand line would try to block him.

Afterward they lined up the same way and practiced tackling.

"Dive with your shoulders against his waist, Freddie," yelled the coach. "At the same time, throw your arms around his knees. Come on! You can do it!"

Freddie did it. But the boy he tackled was a little smaller than himself. Maybe the coach had arranged it that way.

Then the boys practiced blocking. This was mainly a job for the linemen.

Coach Sears said, "Years ago, the Four Horsemen of Notre Dame became famous all over the country. But it was the Seven Mules who helped them become famous. The Seven Mules were their men on the line — those blockers who make up the heart of the team that carries the ball."

While they were learning how to block, Freddie noticed his mom standing with other people at one side of the field. She was wearing her brown coat with the fur collar. They saw each other, and she smiled and waved.

There were a lot of dads there watching, but very few moms. Boy, I wish Dad were alive, thought Freddie.

"Okay!" yelled Coach Sears. "That's all for today. Tomorrow again. Same time. Same place."

The boys began to scatter. Freddie waited for his mom, who was walking toward him. She put her arm around his shoulders and walked with him to the car.

A tall boy about fifteen was standing in front of the Chase's car. He was wearing a maroon jacket with DELMAR printed across the front of it. It was Coach Sears's son, Jeff. He played halfback at Delmar High.

"Hi, Mrs. Chase," he said. "Hi, Freddie."

"Hello, Jeff," said Freddie. "This is Jeff Sears, Mom."

Freddie's mom smiled. "Hello, Jeff. How are you!"

"Good, thanks," said Jeff.

Then Coach Sears came over. He said hi and introduced himself to Mrs. Chase. She shook his hand. She said that she hadn't wanted Freddie to play football, but his father had played, and so she had figured it was all right for Freddie to play since he wanted to so much.

"Freddie's a little afraid of contact yet," said the coach. "But don't worry. He'll make out all right."

Then he went on. "By the way, Spring College is showing a football movie tomorrow night. Jeff and I are going. I was wondering if Freddie might like to join us."

Freddie's face lit up. "Oh! Can I, Mom?"

Mrs. Chase smiled. "I think so," she said. "But remember — school the next day!"

Coach Sears grinned. "He'll be home before nine," he promised. "I'll pick up Freddie about a quarter of seven. Let's go, Jeff. Good night, Freddie — Mrs. Chase."

"Good night, Coach," said Freddie.

The thought of going to the football movie with the coach tomorrow night made Freddie feel important. Maybe things weren't so bad after all.

<u>6</u>

Coach Sears and Jeff stopped by for Freddie a little before a quarter of seven.

The sun had just set behind the hills, leaving a pink sky. Many miles off, Freddie could see the white trails of a jet, like a needle pulling a thread through the clouds.

"Going to be a cold night," observed the coach.

They drove out of the city and began to climb the winding road that would take them to Shelden, and Spring College. They crossed a steel bridge. A narrow river flowed underneath. Freddie saw the sky mirrored in it. He imagined the car flying high in the sky, and just for a moment felt a thrill pass through him.

They turned left past the bridge.

"Colleges show movies like the ones we're going to see tonight all the time," Coach Sears explained. "That way, the players can seem themselves in action. The coach can point out their weaknesses and tell the players how to improve. I thought you guys might enjoy the movie, and also get a few pointers on what halfbacks are supposed to do."

Jeff, who was sitting on the outside with Freddie in the middle, elbowed Freddie. "That's us," he laughed.

Freddie grinned. For a moment he felt a bit important.

The road finally stopped winding, and there ahead of them the lights of Shelden winked in the darkness.

Freddie tapped his foot excitedly as he sat between Coach Sears and Jeff in the hall among all those football players. Coach Sears and the football coach of Spring College, Jim Dickson, had talked to each other awhile just before they sat down, and Freddie decided they must be longtime friends.

The lights were switched off, and the movie started. It showed the opponents running onto the field. Then the Spring College players came on.

38

Everybody in the hall began to clap and some even yelled, but they stopped quickly.

As the teams faced each other on the gridiron, Coach Jim Dickson began to talk.

"This kickoff gave us a good start last week. Bill booted that ball into Penway's end zone. Now watch our defense when Penway takes the ball. Look at that hole through right tackle. See that fullback coming through? But where's our linebacker, number forty-two? That's right, there he is! Making the tackle!"

"Linebackers," whispered Jeff. "That's what we are, Freddie. That is, if you play defense."

Freddie didn't answer. He felt funny all of a sudden. In a game, he should be doing just what that halfback was doing. He should — but he couldn't. He could never tackle like that halfback.

The movie continued. And, as Coach Sears had said, Freddie not only enjoyed it, but he learned a few things, too, he guessed. Maybe — just maybe — it might help him be a better tackler.

Jeff did a lot of talking on the way home. He talked about the movie and about his own high school game last Saturday. He played both offense and defense, and the more Freddie heard him, the more he wished he could be like Jeff. Jeff told about the big guys he tackled, and the big guys he blocked. A guy couldn't be scared of anything if he could do all those things.

They started down the winding road. The headlights of the coach's car picked out the tall trees and the white posts.

The coach made a turn in the road. There ahead was the bridge.

Coming down the grade straight ahead of them was a trailer truck. Its headlights blazed like two glaring eyes, and its horn was blaring.

"Dad!" Jeff screamed. "That truck! It's out of control! It's coming right at us!"

"Hold on!" cried Coach Sears. "He's traveling sixty at least — and on this narrow road! Either something's gone wrong with the truck, or that driver's gone crazy. If I could only make the bridge!"

"But you can't, Dad!" shouted Jeff. "Dad! He's going to hit us!"

The truck was hurling toward them, weaving crazily back and forth across the road. In a second . . .

Coach Sears swung the wheel of the car. There was a crash of metal and stone. Their car bounced like a ball down the hill.

Freddie closed his eyes as tight as he could. He gripped Jeff's arm with one hand and put his other hand against the dashboard.

An instant later there was a resounding splash as the car plunged into the river.

7

The car stood tilted at the bottom of the river. Its left side was higher than its right. Freddie heard nothing but the awful sound of running water. It came from all around them, loud and hissing.

In front, the headlights pierced the watery wall. Less than five feet ahead loomed a tall boulder, standing like a guard against anyone who dared to go past.

The motor was dead. Coach Sears flicked off the ignition key.

Suddenly the lights dimmed and went out.

"Freddie, are you all right?" asked the coach.

Freddie's breath came in gasps. "I — I'm all right!"

"How about you, Jeff?"

"I'm all right, too. But Dad, this door won't open! We can't get out!"

43

"Leave that door alone!" shouted his father. Then Coach Sears's voice softened. "It's impossible to push that door open against that pressure, Jeff. We have to wait until the water nearly fills the inside of the car before we can hope to push these doors open."

"What?" Jeff's voice was filled with panic. "If we do that, we'll drown!"

"Don't get panicky," advised his father. "We won't drown. Just be still and listen to me."

Coach Sears spoke calmly, as if he were not afraid at all. Freddie turned toward him in the darkness. Could Jeff be right? Might they drown?

The coach patted Freddie comfortingly on the shoulder. "We'll get out of this," he said. "Don't worry. Just be thankful we got out of the way of that truck."

Something in the coach's voice erased the fear inside Freddie. He closed his eyes and whispered a prayer of thanks for saving them from being hit by that speeding, lurching truck. He trembled. Then he reminded himself of what the coach had said, and it helped him to control himself.

Water crept up through the floor of the car. Freddie felt it rising around his shoes.

"We're going to get mighty wet," said the coach. "And the water's going to be cold. But we'll get out of this all right. Just listen to me, and don't get panicky."

"If we're waiting for the car to fill up with water, why don't we open the windows a little?" asked Jeff.

"I'm waiting in the hope somebody might have seen us driving off into this river and will send some help," said his father. "Once we're out of this car and on top of the water, some assistance from the outside would be a big help."

The water crept higher and higher. It covered their legs, and soon their knees.

Then a light appeared in front of them — a spotlight — from the bridge. It moved about in the water, settled on the boulder a moment, then on their car!

"Look!" cried Jeff. "Somebody did come!"

A second later, water spilled inside the car from the coach's side.

"I've opened the window a little," said Coach Sears, "to let the water come in faster. Freddie, can you swim?"

"Yes," said Freddie.

"Fine. So can Jeff. Take your shoes off now and leave them in the car."

The water reached their necks. The coach pushed the door open.

"Okay, Freddie," he said. "You first. Crawl over me and I'll follow you. Jeff, you follow me. Careful, now. Don't bump your heads."

Freddie crawled over the coach, pushed himself out of the car, and felt himself carried up and away by the river's current. At the same time the spotlight from the bridge shone on him, and he was able to see where he was going.

The next instant a hand pulled at his coat. It was Coach Sears.

Freddie looked beyond the coach. A second spotlight was directed around the area of the car.

He cried to the coach, "Coach Sears! Where's Jeff? I don't see him!"

8

Coach Sears spun in the water. The second spotlight had joined the first and was shining on them, too.

"Shine a light back there!" the coach yelled at the top of his lungs to the men on the bridge. "There's another boy back there!"

He turned quickly to Freddie. "Freddie! Can you make it to shore by yourself? There are only a few feet to go."

"Yes!" said Freddie. "I can make it! You go after Jeff!"

A man's voice spoke from nearby. "Come over here, son. We'll get you out."

Freddie looked and saw two men standing on shore. One was holding a dim flashlight.

Freddie trembled from the cold and struck out toward the men with hard overhand strokes. But the

47

swift current pushed him downstream like a piece of driftwood. He knew he would never make it.

He tried to yell to them. But water swirled in his face, and he couldn't.

One of the men jumped into the water. He waded into it as far as he could, reached out, and clutched Freddie by an arm. Pulling him in to shallower water, he lifted Freddie to his feet and helped him to shore.

"Thank God!" the man whispered.

He started to carry Freddie up the steep, rocky bank.

"Wait!" Freddie shouted. "Please wait! I have to see if Coach Sears is going to get Jeff!"

The man paused. They both looked up the river, where a spotlight was shining on the water. Freddie saw only one person, the coach, and tears sprang in his eyes.

And then he saw another. Jeff and his father were swimming side by side, heading toward shore.

"All right!" Freddie whispered happily.

Then, in spite of the cold water gnawing at his body, making him shiver like a leaf, a warm feeling filled him.

"O—okay!" he said, his teeth chattering. "Y-you can t-take me up now."

In the game against the Owls on Saturday, Freddie waved to Jeff standing near the sideline among the spectators. Jeff grinned and waved back. They had had an experience neither one of them would forget as long as he lived.

Freddie would never forget that truck driver, either. He was the one who had pulled Freddie out of the river and carried him up to the waiting ambulance. Other drivers, including one with a spotlight, had come along in the meantime and had stopped to help.

"Those brakes," the truck driver had kept saying. "They broke loose coming down that hill. And I couldn't do anything! Anything at all!"

Freddie, Jeff, and Coach Sears had spent the next twenty-four hours in the hospital. The doctor who released them said, "You're all fine. Go home. But get a good rest before that game Saturday."

Freddie's mom was still nervous about it. Freddie had been afraid that she would blame the coach, because Coach Sears had invited him to go to that football movie. But she didn't blame anyone. Not even the truck driver. She could tell that the truck driver was an honest man, she'd said, and if he said that the brakes had failed, then the brakes must have failed.

The next day a crew of men had pulled the coach's car out of the river. It had some bent parts — the fenders and the front axle — but the garage men had promised Coach Sears they'd fix it up and have it running in a week. That surprised Freddie. He had never thought they could lift it out of the river — let alone fix it. But it seemed people could do some pretty amazing things when they put their minds to it.

One person stuck in his memory all through the whole thing. That was Jeff. In the car, Jeff had been scared as anything. A lot more scared than Freddie. And yet on a football field, Jeff could tackle a runner with no fear whatever. And it made no difference how big that runner was.

To Freddie, a runner coming at him was like a freight train.

Of course, that experience in the car was lots more dangerous than playing football. But the coach had helped Freddie remain calm. Look at the trouble he had had trying to calm Jeff.

Bet even little Jimmie Rose wouldn't have been as scared as Jeff was.

Guess different things can put an awful lot of scare in different people, Freddie thought.

From the bench, Freddie watched the Owls' right halfback, Buddy Camp, take a pitchout from the quarterback and race wide around his right end. He got by Joey, then he tried to stiff-arm Bucky Jensen. But Bucky dived at him and knocked Buddy out of bounds.

The Owls had gained about fifteen yards on the play. With the ball on the Sandpipers' twenty-eight-yard line, the Owls pushed forward to the Sandpipers' eight.

Then they tried a pass. It would have worked fine, except that the pass was too short and Ted Butler was there to intercept it. He carried the ball back to his seventeen.

Freddie went in. He carried the ball twice, totaling gains of eight yards. On the third down, Dick Connors completed a forward pass to Joey Mills — but a flag was dropped on the ground.

51

"Holding!" shouted the referee. He signaled by clutching his left arm with his right hand.

"On who?" cried Dick angrily.

The referee pointed at Dave Summers, then marched off fifteen yards against them.

Dick groaned. The penalty put the ball on their ten. Now it was third and seventeen to go.

Dick tried a quarterback sneak and was thrown for a three-yard loss.

"Nothing to do now but kick," he said hopelessly.

Bucky Jensen took the snap back in his end zone, punted it, and then — *smack!* The ball was blocked!

It bounced crazily into the playing zone. An Owls player scooped it up and ran it across the goal line, and the referee shot up both hands.

A touchdown!

They tried for the extra point but missed.

Freddie felt sick. The score was now 12–0 in the Owls' favor, and it was almost the end of the third quarter.

9

After three plays, the quarter was over. The teams exchanged goals. The ball was on the Sandpipers' twenty-two-yard line. Last down and two to go.

Dick Connors shook his head sadly as he and his teammates went into a huddle. Every eye was on him, waiting anxiously for him to decide on what play to use next. He named a play, then changed his mind. He suggested punting but changed his mind again.

"No. We'll give up the ball then," he said. "We've got to hang on to it. Maybe a pass —"

The whistle shrilled. The boys straightened like puppets and stared at the referee.

"Too long in the huddle!" the official said.

He penalized them five yards for delaying the game.

"We'd better get going," said Stookie, "or penalties will put us in our end zone."

"All right," said Dick. "Let's go with play twenty-three! On the two!"

Twenty-three? Freddie rubbed his palms against his sides. Here was his chance.

The ball was on the Sandpipers' seventeen-yard line. There were seven yards to go for a first down. Dick called signals.

"Down! One! Two! Hike!"

Stookie snapped the ball. Dick drew back and handed off to Bucky. Bucky raced toward left end. Dave Summers threw a body block on his man, but Joey's man brushed by Joey and started to reach for Bucky. Just then Bucky pitched the ball out to Freddie. Freddie pulled it against him and began crossing the white stripes as fast as his legs could carry him. He zipped past the twenty, the thirty, the forty. . . .

Now he was in the Owls' territory and still going. He heard someone coming up behind him and tried to pick up more speed.

A pair of arms circled his waist. He was brought down. When he got up, he saw that his tackler was Buddy Camp, the fastest man on the Owls' team.

"Thataway to run, Freddie!" Dick slapped him happily on the back.

Freddie smiled. "Bucky pitched it to me just in time," he said.

The ball was on the Owls' twenty-eight. First down and ten.

"Thirteen flare," said Dick in the huddle.

Thirteen flare was a pass to either right halfback Freddie or left halfback Bucky. It depended on who was in the better position to receive.

The signal. The snap. Dick went back. The Owls' strong lineman plowed through. Dennis blocked a man charging at Dick, but another man was ready to tackle the quarterback.

Dick yanked his arm back and threw. The ball sailed through the air. It was a poor pass; the ball was wobbling crazily — far short of the man for whom it was intended, Bucky Jensen.

Then — just before the ball was about to hit the ground — Joey Mills caught it! He was off balance and almost stumbled to his knees as he tried to hold the ball in his hands. Then he regained his balance and ran hard down the field. Bucky blocked the man near him, and Joey had the field to himself.

He went over for a touchdown. A few seconds later, the Sandpipers bucked the line for the extra point.

The score: Owls 12; Sandpipers 7.

Freddie went out as the Owls became the offensive team. They began threatening with passes and line bucks. A fumble put the ball back in the Sandpipers' possession, and once again Freddie saw action.

Time was running short.

The ball was on the Sandpipers' thirty-one. First and ten.

"Twenty-three!" said Dick in the huddle.

Freddie stared. It was that same play — when he had gone for that real long run. Would it work again?

The signal. The snap. Then Dick trotting back with the ball. He handed it to Bucky. Bucky plowed through a hole between left end and left tackle. Just as a linebacker was ready to hit him, he pitched the ball out to Freddie.

Freddie caught it. He raced forward, hugging the ball against him. On the Owls' twenty-two, he was hit.

It had worked again!

The Sandpipers continued to use running plays. When you're going good on the ground, Coach Sears had reminded them, keep going that way. Don't pass. Somebody might intercept.

Then Dick fumbled — and the Owls recovered. Well, the Owls got the ball, anyway.

Freddie went out again. He didn't have a chance to get back in. The clock ran out with the ball in the Owls' possession, and the game in the Owls' pocket.

Freddie walked home after the game, thinking a lot about it. If he'd only gone past that safety man, he'd have put the Sandpipers ahead. Now it was just another loss.

He heard a yell. It came from ahead of him. He looked up and saw two boys quarreling. One boy was real tall. The other one was real little. The little one was Jimmie Rose.

"Give 'em back to me! They're mine!" Jimmie was crying.

Freddie hurried toward them. He saw something in the tall boy's hands that looked like cards.

"He's got my football player cards, Freddie!" Jimmie yelled. "He won't give 'em back to me!"

"Give them back to him," ordered Freddie.

The tall boy looked at him, laughed, and started to run down the street.

Freddie dropped his helmet near Jimmie and raced after the boy. The boy was taller, but Freddie was faster. Freddie caught up with him. He dived and hit the boy with his shoulder. He wrapped his arms around the boy's waist and brought him down hard.

Freddie got up quickly. With his feet on either side of the boy's stomach, he snapped, "Hand me those cards!"

The boy clamped his lips tightly together and handed Freddie the cards. Freddie stepped back, turned, and gave the cards to his little friend Jimmie. The tall boy rose to his feet and ran off down the street.

Jimmie wiped the tears from his eyes and grinned proudly at his friend Freddie. "Thanks, Freddie! You really tackled him, didn't you?"

Freddie looked at Jimmie. Sudden joy bubbled inside him. That's right! He had, hadn't he?

He had really tackled that bully!

10

"We're having a Halloween party at my house," Dick Connors said after practice the next day. "Everybody's going to be dressed in costume. Would you like to come?"

Freddie stared, feeling both happy and surprised. Dick inviting him to a Halloween party? He had thought that the only time Dick ever noticed him was at a football game.

But he couldn't say no. Dick was more than just captain of the Sandpipers. He was popular in school. He played trumpet in the school band, and last year he had made the honor roll every quarter.

"Sure, I'll come," said Freddie. "Thanks!"

"Don't forget. Be dressed in costume," reminded Dick.

"I won't forget," promised Freddie.

Freddie was so pleased, he smiled the whole way home without realizing it. He felt important and proud.

But what costume would he wear? He didn't have any!

The smile vanished, and he didn't feel so important and proud anymore. If his mom didn't buy him a costume, he'd have to tell Dick he couldn't go to the party. Dick would tell the other guys. Imagine, then, what they'd say about Freddie!

He reached home, but it wasn't until long after suppertime that he told his mom about the invitation. Her eyes brightened, and her lips curved in a warm smile.

"The only thing is, Mom," explained Freddie, his heart pounding, "everybody will be wearing costumes. And I don't have one."

"So?" said Mom. "We'll get you one!"

"You will?" Freddie's eyes popped wide as plums. "But they cost money, Mom! Don't they?"

"Yes. But we don't have to spend too much for one." She laughed. "Let's see. What kind do you like?

After a lot of talking and thinking, Freddie decided he'd like to have a pirate costume.

"A pirate it is," Mom said.

She came home with one the next day. It fit Freddie perfectly. She also bought him a mask, which covered the top half of his face.

He was wearing the costume when a knock sounded on the door. Quickly he ran to his room. Mom's laughter trailed after him.

You can laugh, Mom, he thought. But nobody's going to know who's wearing this costume until the party!

He removed his costume and hung it in the closet. Then he returned to the living room. Sitting in an armchair was Mrs. Rose, Jimmie's mother. She had the wide collar of her coat off her shoulders, and her hands folded in her lap.

"Hello, Freddie," she said. "I want to thank you for coming to Jimmie's rescue. He told me about the trouble he had with that boy."

"What trouble?" Mom said. She looked puzzled, and Mrs. Rose went on to tell her exactly what had happened. Jimmie, Freddie realized, hadn't left out a single detail in telling his mom the story.

"You know, he looks up to you," said Mrs. Rose. "Matter of fact, he says you're the best football player in the whole league and wants to play like you when he gets bigger."

She laughed, and added, "He wants me to ask you something, Freddie. He would like very much to have you go trick or treating with him tomorrow night."

Freddie's jaw dropped. "I can't! I mean — I'm going to a Halloween party —" He stopped, wet his lips. His face was flushed.

Mrs. Rose's smile faded slightly. "Oh. You're going to a party?"

"I — I was invited," said Freddie.

Mrs. Rose's smile returned quickly, but Freddie could tell it wasn't real. "Then you keep your invitation," she said. "Someone else can take Jimmie. There's Richard a few doors away from us. And Peter —"

"No, no!" Freddie interrupted. "I'll go with him trick or treating. I don't have to go to the party."

"Don't be silly, Freddie," said Mrs. Rose. "You go to the party."

She stood up, pulled her coat snugly over her shoulders, and started toward the door.

"Don't worry about it, Freddie." Her smile still didn't look real. "You have accepted the invitation to the party. It's only fair that you keep it."

Just then somebody turned the knob of the door on the outside. The door opened, and in came Jimmie. A smile a mile wide was on his face as he looked up at his mother and then at Freddie. His big blue eyes sparkled brightly.

"Hi, everybody!" he cried. "Hi, Freddie! Going trick or treating with me tomorrow night?"

11

Freddie stared at Jimmie and nodded. "Sure, Jimmie! Sure, I'll go with you!"

But his mind was crying out to him — What will Dick say? And what about the next game, and the next? He probably won't let me carry the ball again. But look at Jimmie. That little guy looks up to me! I can't refuse him!

"Thanks, Freddie!" said Jimmie, his eyes bright as stars. "I told Mom you would!"

"Jimmie," Mrs. Rose said softly, "Freddie can't take you tomorrow night. He's been invited to a Halloween party."

The brightness disappeared from Jimmie's eyes. Disappointment came over his face. "But he just said —"

"He wants to be nice to you," Mrs. Rose said. She took Jimmie's hand and opened the door. "Come on, Jimmie. And don't feel bad about it. Freddie didn't know you wanted him to go trick or treating with you, or he wouldn't have promised to go to that party."

"But Mrs. Rose!" pleaded Freddie. "I said I'd go with him!"

She smiled. "I know, Freddie. But please don't let this worry you. I'll find someone for Jimmie. Good night, now. Good night, Mary."

The door closed behind them, and Freddie turned around and looked at his mom. A smile tugged at her lips, and she shrugged.

"You do what you like, Freddie," she said.

The next night, he dressed in his pirate's costume, put on his mask, and went over to Jimmie's house. He rang the bell. Mrs. Rose answered the door.

"Hello, Mrs. Rose," said Freddie. His lips spread in a smile below his mask. "I came to take Jimmie trick or treating."

Her eyes widened. She stared at Freddie and at his costume. For a long minute she acted as if she didn't know just what to say.

Then Jimmie came running forward. He ducked under his mom's arm and cracked a big smile at Freddie.

"Hey! A pirate!" he cried. "Are you trick or treating?"

"I'm Freddie," said Freddie. "I've come to take you trick or treating. Don't you have a costume?"

"Freddie?" Jimmie's face brightened like a jack-o'-lantern. "You bet I do! I'll be in it in no time!"

Mrs. Rose invited Freddie into the house. It didn't take long for Jimmie to dress in his costume, a black cat suit with whiskers, pointed ears, and a long tail. Mrs. Rose gave him a paper sack, and together he and Freddie went out the door and down the street.

They stopped at each house, and Freddie let Jimmie either knock or press the doorbell. "Trick or treat!" Jimmie would say, and whoever answered would almost always have something ready to put into the sack. A candy bar, pieces of caramel, packages of nuts or jelly beans.

"Thank you!" Jimmie would reply.

He's really enjoying this, thought Freddie. I guess I did the right thing by coming with him.

Finally they came to a house Freddie recognized immediately. It was big and white, with a hedge along the walk and tall lilac bushes guarding the front porch steps. This was where Dick Connors lived. Freddie saw figures in costume passing back and forth in front of the lighted windows.

"Let's not stop here, Jimmie," said Freddie hastily. "They seem to have a lot of company."

"That's all right!" said Jimmie. "Let's go anyway!"

Freddie laughed at Jimmie's spunkiness, shook his head, and followed the little boy up the steps to the front door. Jimmie pressed a button. Soon the door opened and a boy in a tiger's costume looked out at them.

"Trick or treat!" said Jimmie.

"Well, look at this!" the boy said, and pulled the door open wider. "Come on in and join our party!"

Freddie recognized that voice instantly. The boy was Dick Connors.

Jimmie stepped inside. Freddie followed him. The room was filled with boys and girls in costume. They all had their masks on their faces so that it was practically impossible to tell who they were.

Some of them began putting fruit and candy into Jimmie's sack. Somebody in a white rabbit's costume put a colored paper hat on Jimmie's head, and somebody else tied a blue ribbon around the end of his tail. They were having a good time, and Jimmie was laughing happily with them.

Then a tall boy stepped in front of Freddie. He wore a funny mask that completely covered his face and muffled his voice when he spoke.

"You look familiar," he said. Then, before Freddie could protect himself, the boy lifted his mask.

"Well, look who we have here!" He suddenly let go of the mask. It snapped back against Freddie's forehead.

Freddie, stunned and angry, yanked his mask back down over his eyes and went to the door. "Come on, Jimmie!" he said. "Let's get out of here!"

"You shouldn't have done that!" Dick Connors snapped at the boy who had lifted Freddie's mask. "Look what you did. You hurt him. How would you like to have somebody do that to you?"

"Okay," the boy answered. "I'm sorry. He didn't have to get mad about it."

Freddie and Jimmie left quickly.

Freddie could make only a guess, but he had a good idea who that boy was who had lifted his mask.

Mert McGuire. His own cousin.

<u>12</u>

At eleven o'clock the next morning, on the A field, the Sandpipers kicked off to the Bluejays. At the same time, on the B field, the Flamingos kicked off to the Cardinals. Until today the Cardinals had won two games and lost one; the Sandpipers had lost two and tied one. They had yet to win a game.

Like small armies, the Sandpipers and the Bluejays rushed at each other. The Sandpipers were in canary yellow, the Bluejays in powder blue.

The Bluejays' flashy fullback, Art Neeley, caught the kick and ran it back to his twenty-two.

Freddie waited for Ted Butler, or somebody, to come in and take his place in the linebacker slot. But no one rushed in from the Sandpipers' bench. At last he was being given another chance on defense!

71

The Bluejays hurried out of their huddle. With a wingback playing a few feet behind and to the right of their right end, the Bluejays' quarterback began snapping signals.

"Down! Set! One! Two!"

The quarterback took the snap. He hurried back and handed off to Art Neeley. The Sandpipers' line broke through. Freddie sidestepped a husky tackle and rushed through a hole after Neeley. But Neeley was sweeping around his right end, the ball tucked under his arm.

He plunged past Joey Mills and crossed the line of scrimmage. It looked as if he was really on his way. Dave Summers, one of the fastest linemen on the team, raced after him. He caught Neeley's arm. Neeley tried to get away. Bucky Jensen rushed forward and tackled him.

The Bluejays had gained twelve yards on the play. Once again it was first down for them.

The ball was on their thirty-four-yard line. Again Neeley carried the ball. This time he plunged through left tackle — directly toward Freddie.

For a fraction of a second, panic overcame Freddie. Art Neeley was coming *toward* him — he wasn't running *away* from him, not like that boy who had taken little Jimmie's cards. This was different.

He had to stop Neeley. He couldn't let him get by.

Right tackle Steve Cook grabbed Neeley, who shook himself loose and looked directly into Freddie's eyes. A grin came over his lips, as if he were defying Freddie. He pushed out his right hand. Quick as lightning, Freddie ducked and wrapped his arms around the fullback's knees.

Neeley went down!

The players piled on Neeley and Freddie. The referee's whistle shrilled, and the players unpiled. Freddie and Neeley were the last to get up.

He met Neeley's eyes again. This time there was a sort of respectful look in Neeley's gaze. He had gained only two yards.

On the second down, the Bluejays tried a criss-cross buck. The quarterback faked to the left half-back, then handed the ball to the right halfback. The halfback plunged toward the hole in the right side of the Sandpipers' line.

Freddie and Harry Lott hit him, tackling him a yard behind scrimmage.

Both Freddie and Harry rose, smiling at each other.

"Way to go, Freddie!" Dick Connors said. "You're doing it now!"

The Bluejays gained three yards on the next play. They punted on the fourth.

Bucky Jensen caught the ball on his thirty and carried it to the thirty-six.

"Twelve pass," said Dick in the huddle.

Twelve meant that Dick was to pass to Bucky. They tried it, but Neeley knocked down the ball. Neeley seemed to be everywhere.

Dennis plowed through tackle for a seven-yard gain, and Freddie flashed around right end for six more yards and a first down.

The Sandpipers began moving, pushing the ball closer and closer toward the Bluejays' goal line.

Then, on a double reverse, Dick handed off to Bucky and Bucky to Freddie.

Freddie fumbled! A Bluejay fell on the ball, and the Sandpipers' chances to score a touchdown vanished.

13

For a while the Sandpipers' spirits sank. Their shoulders and chins sagged. Dick slapped his helmet against his side disgustedly and shot a dark look out of the corner of his eye at Freddie.

Freddie felt the others glare at him, too. He couldn't blame them. It was his fault, and he wished that Coach Sears would take him out.

That double reverse was a good surprise play. It could have worked fine. With only thirteen yards to go for a goal, the Sandpipers might have scored a touchdown.

The Bluejays hustled to the scrimmage line, and Freddie trotted to his linebacker spot. Apparently Coach Sears wanted him to remain in there.

The Bluejays tried an end-around run. It worked for an eight-yard gain. Then a halfback plunged through tackle, and it was Freddie who brought him down. The Bluejays made first down on their next play, and the quarter ended. The teams switched goals.

Twice the Bluejays made first downs, gaining ground on passes and line bucks. Then they lost ground on a five-yard penalty charge; one of their players was offside. They couldn't regain the loss, and the ball went to the Sandpipers.

The Sandpipers moved forward slowly. Then Dick shot a quick pass to Joey Mills. But it wasn't Joey who caught the ball. Swift as a bird, Art Neeley swooped in, intercepted it, and went all the way for a touchdown!

Then he scored the extra point.

Freddie could hear the Bluejay fans cheering from the sidelines and the bleachers. Cheering for Art Neeley.

The Bluejays kicked off to the Sandpipers. And now the Sandpipers tried to hold on to the ball, tried hard to gain those ten yards in order to keep going. Freddie's runs through tackle and around the ends, and Dennis Yates's hard plunges, were bringing them closer to the Bluejays' end zone. Not even two offside penalties dimmed the Sandpipers' hopes.

Then Dick fumbled a snap from center, and a Bluejay pounced on the ball!

That did it!

The Bluejays tried pushing the ball the other way. On their own thirty-five, Harry Lott was charged for holding, which gave the Bluejays fifteen more yards.

Freddie shook his head unhappily. It would be like Harry to do such a thing.

The Bluejays tried a surprise play. The quarterback handed off to Art Neeley. Art started running toward the side, then quickly shot a pass. But the Sandpiper safety got under the wobbling ball, caught it, and sprinted down the field!

He crossed the goal line for a TD, and Dennis bucked the line for the extra point.

Now the score was tied.

The game remained tied until the middle of the third quarter, when the Bluejays had the ball on the Sandpipers' fifteen-yard line. With five yards to go on the fourth down, Neeley went into position to kick a field goal. The ball shot straight between the uprights, and the Bluejays went ahead, 10–7.

Once again the Sandpipers lost hope, letting their shoulders droop and their chins sag.

"Come on, you guys!" Freddie could hear Coach Sears yelling. "Get in there and fight! You can do it!"

Freddie had a glimpse of his mom, too. She was sitting in the third row of the bleachers with other moms and dads.

Bet she knows more about football than a lot of those women, Freddie thought. She had learned it when she used to watch Dad play. Gee, if only Dad could be here . . .

The Sandpipers could do very little. Coach Sears made replacements. Ted went in for Freddie.

"We could have been far ahead in this game," said Coach Sears, "if we had kept our wits about us. We have this game to play, and the one with the Cardinals next week. Don't you want to win?"

Freddie remembered those words when he got back into the game. But it wasn't until just after the start of the fourth quarter that his opportunity came. Once more it was on a double reverse. This time he took the ball from Bucky without trouble, swept around left end, and went all the way.

Dennis bucked for the point, and the score was Sandpipers 14, Bluejays 10.

Later, when the Bluejays had the ball, Freddie was taken out. He went in again only when the Sandpipers got the ball. He realized after this happened the third time that Coach Sears was playing him only on offense.

What have I done now? he asked himself worriedly.

He looked over at the other field and noticed that the Cardinals-Flamingos game was over; that some of the players were here, watching this game. Among them was his cousin Mert.

There was time for only a few more plays. The Bluejays had the ball on the Sandpipers' thirty-six. They tried a short pass and gained eight yards. Then Neeley broke lose on a play around left end — and went fifteen yards!

Freddie fidgeted on the bench. He looked at Coach Sears. The coach glanced at his watch, then began rubbing his knees nervously.

The Bluejays tried a line buck. No gain.

"Hold them, line! Hold them!" yelled the Sandpipers' fans.

Again Neeley carried the ball, going around his right end this time. *Get him, somebody!* Freddie wanted to shout. *Get him!*

It was Dennis who pulled Neeley down — on the five-yard line.

Then the whistle shrilled. The game was over.

"Whew! Just in time!" murmured Freddie.

The Sandpipers were the winners: 14–10.

The boys leaped and hugged each other with joy they had not known in a long, long time. This was their first win in two years!

Jimmie walked alongside Freddie on their way home, talking every minute and telling Freddie how wonderfully he played and what a great run that was.

"Fifty-five yards!" said Jimmie, and whistled.

Fifty-five yards? Freddie smiled. He hadn't realized what it was at the time.

Then along his other side approached Mert, carrying his helmet.

"Well, see you guys finally won a game," he said. "And I heard you made a TD, Freddie. Congratulations!

"Thanks," said Freddie. "How did you make out?"

"We won. Thirty-nine to thirteen. I made three touchdowns."

"You did?"

"I heard you made some nice tackles," Mert went on. "Must be just talk. The coach was taking you out every time on defense while I was watching the game."

"We play you next week," Freddie said. "You'll have a better chance to watch me then."

Mert chuckled. "It's a deal!" he said. "But I think it'll be an easy win — for us!" He ran off ahead of them, his laughter trailing behind him.

Don't be too sure, thought Freddie. I'll have my chance to pay you back for what you did to me at Dick Connors's Halloween party!

14

For the next several days, the important subject around school was the Sandpipers' win over the Bluejays. The Monday *Evening Times* had an article describing the highlights of the game. Freddie cut it out and pasted it in his scrapbook among his other clippings.

This article contained a special piece about him. Freddie was proud, but he didn't brag about it the way his cousin Mert bragged about his write-ups.

"Special praise is deserved by Freddie Chase, the Sandpipers' right halfback," one paragraph read. "His sparkling runs through the line and around the ends were a sight to see. Several times he shook off tacklers for sizable gains. He proved himself on defense, too, tackling big, fast runners such as Art

Neeley, the Bluejays' star fullback. But his most spectacular play was his fifty-five-yard touchdown run. . . ."

Little by little the conversation among the football fans drifted to this coming Saturday's game between the Sandpipers and the Cardinals. Almost everybody felt that it was going to be an easy victory for the Cardinals. Almost everybody . . . except the Sandpipers.

"Just wait and see," said Mert McGuire, smiling with lots of confidence. "We'll run through you Sandpipers so bad, there won't be a feather left on you!"

Freddie expected Mert to say something about that night at Dick Connors's party. But Mert didn't. Either he had forgotten the incident or he didn't want Freddie to know that it was he who had lifted Freddie's mask.

But Freddie knew. And Saturday the Cardinals' red feathers would be flying, not the Sandpipers' yellow ones.

For Thursday, Freddie's English class had to write compositions — on any subject. Freddie wrote his on Wednesday night. He titled it THE BIG GAME. It was a story about a football game between the Sandpipers and the Cardinals. He made up the names of the players, but he was thinking of some real live people while he wrote.

According to his story, the game ended with the Sandpipers shutting out the Cardinals, 14–0.

As Miss Daley handed Freddie's paper back to him, a smile curled her lips. Freddie blushed, took the paper, and glanced quickly at the mark in the upper right-hand corner.

An *A!*

Freddie grinned.

Coach Sears had the Sandpipers work out Tuesday, Wednesday, and Thursday. He drilled them on passes, line bucks, and the double reverse.

"The Cardinals have the strongest team in the league," he reminded his charges after practice Thursday evening. "But they just eased by the Bluejays, and the Catbirds beat them, twenty-eight to twenty-seven. And we tied the Catbirds. I know that doesn't mean much, but it does mean they could be beaten. Just make up your minds that you can do it. Play as hard as you can, and you will. Remember this: If the Cardinals win, they'll get in first place for sure. If they lose, they may end in third. And it will be the first time they haven't finished on top in three years! Okay. Scatter! See you Saturday afternoon!"

Freddie and Jimmie watched part of the Flamingo-Catbird game and part of the Owl-Bluejay game on Saturday morning. Both matchups were filled with excitement. The Catbirds won, 28–19; the Owls and the Bluejays tied, 7–7.

After leaving Jimmie, Freddie went home and looked over the records of all the teams. After this morning's two games, the Cardinals were still sitting pretty right on top. But if they lost to the Sandpipers this afternoon, they would have two in the lost column. That would put them in third place! The records were as follows:

	Won	Lost	Tied
CARDINALS	3	1	0
OWLS	3	1	1
CATBIRDS	3	1	1

	Won	Lost	Tied
SANDPIPERS	1	2	1
BLUEJAYS	1	3	1
FLAMINGOS	1	4	0

Of course, the Sandpipers would finish in fourth place, but that wasn't as important as knocking off the Cardinals.

Freddie gritted his teeth. We'll knock them off that perch this afternoon! Just watch! We'll show Mert! We'll show them all!

15

The crowd that attended the game that afternoon was the largest Freddie had seen at any of the games. His mom was there with Mert's parents, Mrs. Rose, and Jimmie. You couldn't have kept Jimmie away today!

The sun was hidden behind high gray clouds that moved across the sky like sticky syrup. A light, cool wind made it necessary for the fans to wear coats. For the football players, however, this weather was just dandy.

The whistle shrilled. Mert McGuire, the Cardinals' fullback, kicked off.

Bucky Jensen caught the ball on the fifteen and ran it back to his twenty-seven. In three plays the Sandpipers moved the ball to their thirty-eight for a first down.

"Crisscross buck," said Dick in the huddle. "Freddie takes it!"

Dick took the snap and faked it to Bucky, who scissored across in front of him. Then he handed the ball to Freddie, who scissored in front of him to the left. Freddie sliced through a hole and dodged a tackler. He crossed the Cardinals' thirty-five-yard line and was brought down hard.

"Nice gain," said Mert, who had tackled him. "Let's see you try it again."

"Second and two," said the referee.

Dennis bucked but failed to make it. Then Dick tried a quarterback sneak, taking the ball through the line himself. He made a gain, but there was doubt whether it was a first down. The referee motioned to the men with the yardage chain and down marker for a measurement.

A first down! The Sandpipers' fans roared from the sidelines and the bleachers.

Then the Cardinals seemed to gain strength. They held the Sandpipers and gained possession of the ball on their thirty-one. Freddie was taken out. Ted Butler went in.

Freddie was baffled. Why? he thought. Why has the coach been taking me out when we're on defense?

The Cardinals moved forward slowly. Then their quarterback, Jim Small, shot a lateral to Mert. Mert raced all the way down the field for a touchdown. Jim bucked the line for the extra point, and the Cardinals went into the lead, 7–0.

In the second quarter, the Sandpipers got the ball and Freddie went back in. Mert grinned at him.

Freddie didn't return the grin.

I hope I have the chance to tackle you, he thought. Even if it's only once.

The Sandpipers hit twice with passes that took them to the Cardinals' twelve-yard line. Then a clipping charge against Joey Mills set them back fifteen. Dick tried to hit Freddie with a long pass, hoping to score. But someone stretched long arms in front of Freddie and practically took the ball out of his hands. . . . It was Mert.

The Cardinals' fullback sprinted down the field. He dodged Joey and Dave Summers. At last Freddie tackled him from behind, and Mert went down.

Mert's eyes went wide as he looked around at his tackler.

"Say! Nice tackle!" he said.

He sounded as it he meant it, but Freddie said nothing. He was thinking, There! I've done it. And I'll do it again.

A moment later, Ted Butler came running in. "Out, Freddie," he said.

Freddie stared, wondering why.

The Cardinals wormed their way far into the Sandpipers' territory. Then, on the five-yard line, Jim Small fumbled.

Sandpipers' ball . . . but the Sandpipers had all they could do to keep the ball in their possession during the remaining moments of the second quarter.

Shortly after the first half ended, Freddie approached Coach Sears.

"Coach, can't I play defense, too? I'm sure I can stop those players just as well as anybody."

Coach Sears smiled and winked. "I know you can, Freddie. I took you out from defense during the first half for a definite reason. I didn't want the

Cardinals to know how well you've come along as a tackler. During this second half, they'll find out. But by the time they do, they might not make enough gains to matter beans, and we might have that ball in our possession enough times to beat them. That's peculiar strategy, maybe. But let's hope it works!"

16

The second half was ready to begin. The Sandpipers chose to receive. Mert McGuire kicked off for the Cardinals. It was a low, bouncing ball that went deep into the Sandpipers' territory. Dick Connors tucked it under his arm and started running it back. He barely reached his eighteen-yard line before being tackled.

In three plays, the Sandpipers failed to gain more than five yards. Dennis punted. It was high and not very far. Jim Small signaled for a fair catch. Now the Cardinals had the ball on the Sandpipers' thirty-two.

The Cardinals inched forward. They were discovering something: Few runners were getting past linebacker Freddie Chase.

Then Jim shot a long pass to his right end; the player raced all the way for a TD; Mert bucked from the two-yard line for the extra point.

The Sandpipers groaned.

With two minutes left in the third quarter, Dick took the snap from center Stookie Freese and shot a quick pass to Freddie just over the line of scrimmage. Freddie slipped past a linebacker, dodged Jim Small, and then raced hard down the field. Mert was after him. But Freddie kept ahead of Mert all the way.

He didn't slow down till he crossed the goal line.

Mert puffed behind him. "Boy! Nice run, Freddie! Even if you are my cousin!"

Freddie turned briefly and saw Mert smiling. For a second he grinned back.

"I'm just remembering that Halloween party, that's all," said Freddie, and trotted away.

Dennis tried for the extra point. He didn't make it.

Score: Cardinals 14, Sandpipers 6.

Once again the Cardinals had the ball and began to threaten. From their thirty, they marched to the Sandpipers' eighteen. Then Mert plunged through left tackle and Freddie smeared him.

Like a slippery bean the ball squirted out of Mert's hands! Players in red and yellow scrambled madly for it.

Then — Sandpipers' ball!

Dick threw a lateral to Bucky, and Bucky galloped for a first down. A short pass to Freddie gave them eight more yards. Then, for a moment, the Sandpipers were stopped.

Dick called time.

They rested, wet their dry throats with water a boy fetched them in a bucket, then started again.

They tried two plays and squeezed out another first down just before the third quarter ended.

The teams exchanged goals. The ball was on the Sandpipers' thirty-seven.

"Double reverse," said Dick in the huddle. "Bucky to Freddie."

It worked! Freddie raced around left end for twenty-six yards before he was brought down.

Dick tried a long pass to Joey. It was knocked down. He tried again. The ball sailed out of bounds. Incomplete.

"They won't expect a third pass," said Dick. "A short one to Bucky. Come on. We've got to keep going!"

He took the snap from center, stepped back, and tossed a quick pass to Bucky. The left halfback sprinted for eleven yards.

First down, and six to go for a touchdown.

On the next play, the Sandpipers lost five yards on an offside penalty.

Then, as if he had sprouted wings on his feet, Dennis caught a lateral from Dick and ran the eleven yards for a touchdown.

Dick bucked for the extra point. The Cardinals stopped him.

Score: Cardinals 14, Sandpipers 12.

A moment after the Cardinals returned the kick-off, the referee called time and held up four fingers.

"Four minutes left to play!" said Dick to his team. "Let's get back that ball!"

The Cardinals were stubborn. They didn't try any passes in their first few plays. They knew that an interception could give the Sandpipers a good chance to go for a touchdown.

They moved the ball to the Sandpipers' thirty-eight, then to the thirty. Slowly, with strong moves, they pushed forward to the twenty-four. There the

Sandpipers held as if each player were glued to the next. They were like a yellow brick wall.

With seven yards to go and fourth down, the Cardinals went into punt formation. The Sandpipers fanned out, Dick playing just inside the end zone.

But Mert fooled them! He didn't kick.

Instead, he heaved a long pass to his left end, who was running toward the sideline. The ball was high, spiraling beautifully.

Then something happened. A pair of hands snatched the ball out of the air, inches away from the end's hands. . . .

It was Freddie!

Freddie raced along the sideline. Behind him came the end from whom Freddie had practically stolen the ball. Harder and harder Freddie ran. The smudged white stripes slipped underneath him. Then, on the ten, he was hit. The runner had finally caught up with him.

The referee brought the ball in to the in-bounds line, about thirteen yards from the sideline.

"First, and goal to go!" he cried.

"How many more minutes?" asked Dennis.

"Minutes?" Dick glanced at the referee, then back again. "Forty seconds! Holy catfish! We'll have a chance for only two plays."

"Let's get the ball closer to the middle of the field," suggested Dennis. "Then let me try a field goal."

All eyes swung to him, then back to the captain.

"Okay!" said Dick. "I'll hand off to Freddie. Shoot for the left, Freddie, then charge in! Hurry! We don't have much time!"

Dick snapped signals. Freddie took the hand-off, made a left-end sweep, and was tackled. He gained only a yard, but now the ball was near the center of the field, and nine yards from the goal line. Five yards behind the goal line loomed the goalposts.

"Dennis," said Dick in the huddle, "you'll have to kick that ball at least twenty yards in the air to get it over those crossbars!"

"I know," said Dennis, rubbing his hands on his muddy pants.

They broke out of the huddle. Dick knelt about six yards behind Stookie. He caught the snap and held the ball at a slant for Dennis to kick.

Dennis kicked it squarely. The ball sailed up and over between the uprights. Even before it hit the ground, the whistle shrilled and the game was over.

The Sandpipers had won, 15–14!

Never had the Sandpipers rejoiced as they did then. There were lots of shouts and laughter, and even some happy tears.

"Let me shake your hand, Cousin," Mert said to Freddie, smiling. "You played a wonderful game."

"Thanks," said Freddie "You did, too, Mert."

"Say, what did you mean when you said something to me about a Halloween party? I don't know anything about any Halloween party!"

Freddie stared at him. "You mean you weren't the guy who lifted my mask in front of everybody that night?"

Someone burst out laughing at Freddie's elbow. "Not him, Freddie!" said Dick Connors. "That was Art Neeley. You mean you didn't know?"

Freddie blushed. "No. All the time I thought it was Mert. Gosh — I'm sorry, Cousin. Can you forgive me?"

"Seeing that it's you, I suppose so!" Mert said, laughing.

Freddie laughed, too. Then he wondered: Would he have played so well if he hadn't suspected all the time that it was Mert? But he was glad, now, that it wasn't.

"How about coming over for supper tonight?" Freddie asked. "Mom won't mind."

Mert smiled broadly. "It's a deal!" he said.

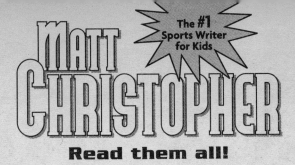

The #1 Sports Writer for Kids

Read them all!

All available in paperback from Little, Brown and Company

Matt Christopher

Sports Bio Bookshelf

Michael Jordan

Steve Young

Grant Hill

Wayne Gretzky

Greg Maddux

Ken Griffey Jr.

Andre Agassi

Mo Vaughn

Emmitt Smith

Hakeem Olajuwon

Tiger Woods

Randy Johnson